HARRY HUGGER AND FIELD TRIP FRIDAY

What happens when Harry and his friends meet some animals who are definitely different?

Dedicated to

the belief that there are no strangers in the world.

There are only friends we have not gotten to know, yet.

Inspired by

Taylor, Grayson and Paula

Editors

Madi Foley and Mark Ramsay

Associate Editors

Annabelle, Simon, Harrison and Veronica

Maxton, Corbin and Logan

Harry woke up early. He could not sleep because it was Field Trip Friday.

This was Harry's favorite school day. He hurriedly followed his morning routine. He brushed his teeth, combed his hair and ate a breakfast of fresh fruit.

Harry picked out an extra special bow tie.
On a special day like today, everyone would be
dapperly dressed.

His parents were now awake. Using his hugging superpower, he hugged his tiny merry Mom and his big daring Dad.

Harry hugged sister Harriet and helped her find her blue backpack.

Harry rushed out to catch the bus. Since he had gotten up so early, it was a long, weird wait.

At school, Harry hugged his hug-friendly friends.
Harry hugged his talkative teacher.

After listening to some announcements, the talkative teacher told them that today they would be going to Play Park.

As a special treat, they would be meeting another class from a school in a different district next to Play Park.

Before long, the bus with Harry and his class arrived at Play Park. They were so excited that they were having trouble sitting in their separate seats.

As they got off the bus, Harry's class could see the class from the other school coming outside and heading toward Play Park.

Harry's classmates watched, becoming quiet when they realized the other class was not made up of happy hamsters.

They weren't hamsters. They were different –
different colors, different clothes and different
faces. They were definitely different.

Harry's classmates became quiet and began to draw closer together. The other class's talking suddenly stopped as well, and the quiet turned awkwardly awful.

Harry thought about what his merry Mom had always said: "Someone may look different on the outside, however, on the inside, everyone has the same daring dreams, frightening fears and high hopes."

Then Harry thought about what his daring Dad told him: "Being brave is when you put your fear aside and do what you know is really right."

Harry hoped Mom and Dad were right. He adjusted his bow tie, remembered his superpower, put one foot in front of the other and slowly walked toward the curious class.

He stopped a few feet from the strangers. He smiled and opened his arms. Everyone's eyes were on him. He was all alone.

A long moment passed and one brave bunny from the new class took a step forcefully forward.

The brave bunny opened his arms. Harry and the brave bunny gave each other a huge hug.

Slowly, both classes moved toward each other. The brave bunny's name was Barry. Barry introduced Harry to his best friend. Harry's best friend joined Harry and Barry. Soon the classes were marvelously mingling.

The rest of the day was spent making new friends, learning new games and sharing stories.

Barry taught Harry's classmates how to play bunny ball. When they were done playing, Barry gave Harry his cool carrotbat.

Harry taught Barry and his friends how to play
hamster hide-and-seek.

They ate lunch together and shared with each other new, fantastic foods.

The day went by fast, and soon it was time to exchange heartfelt hugs and grinning goodbyes.

When Harry got home, he shared the story with his family. Merry Mom and daring Dad were proud parents.

At the end of the day, Harry and his family had a great group hug. Harry, Harriet, Mom and Dad wrapped their arms around each other and squeezed tightly. It was the best way to end fun Friday.

Lying in bed, Harry hugged himself. Harry had been brave and strong. His hugging superpower had made him a lot of new, fun friends and his world was boldly better.

Tomorrow would be a super Saturday.

---The Beginning---

Made in the USA
Monee, IL
07 November 2020